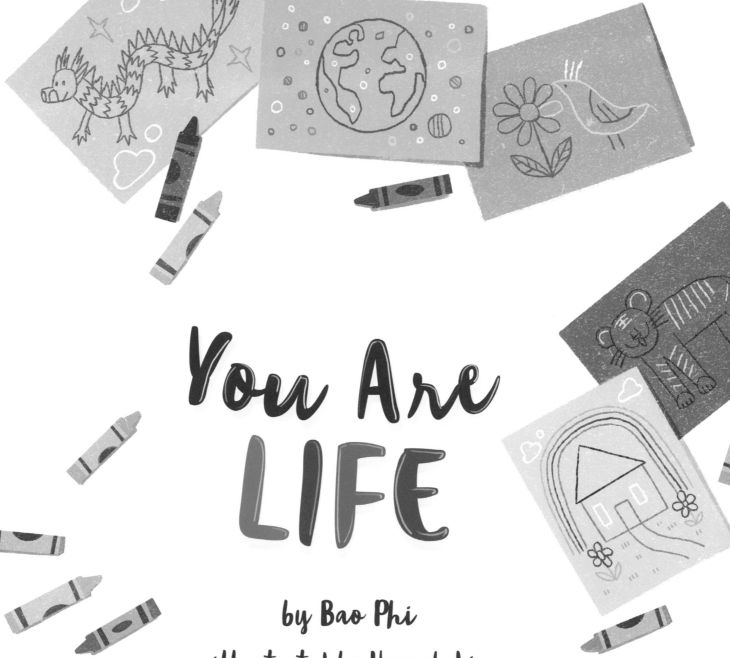

You Are
LIFE

by Bao Phi

illustrated by Hannah Li

CAPSTONE EDITIONS
a capstone imprint

Published by Capstone Editions, an imprint of Capstone.
1710 Roe Crest Drive
North Mankato, Minnesota 56003
capstonepub.com

Library of Congress Cataloging-in-Publication Data is available on the Library of Congress website.
ISBN: 9781684464821 (hardcover)
ISBN: 9781684465095 (eBook PDF)

Summary: Every child is full to bursting with amazing things! This joyful poem celebrates the wonderful and complex identities of children of immigrants and refugees, embracing all that they are—a dancer, a shining light, a K-pop song—and promising what they will never be: invisible. Through lyrical text and fantastical illustrations, award-winning picture book author and poet Bao Phi and illustrator Hannah Li remind young readers that who they are and what they love will always be enough.

Image Credits:
Bao Phi author photo: Anna Min

Designer: Kay Fraser

A note about the text:
In Vietnamese, ông nội means paternal grandfather, and bà nội means paternal grandmother.

For my people, and for yours —BP

To the lighthouse of my life, my baba
and mama, Li Limin and Huo Hong —HL

You are life.
A raft. A lighthouse.
An outstretched hand.

You are not a virus.
You are a seed.
When you were born, you saved me.

You are not forever foreign.
You are Immigrant.

Born here.
Adopted.
Refugee, you fled a war.

You are a Dance Dance Revolution in a field of rice.
You are an ancestral dance flash mob in a mega mall
parking lot.

You are singing along to Korean pop songs,
  dancing along to a Bollywood scene.
You are a language lost.

You are not a burden.
In a basket of arms, you are the most precious thing.

You are not an invader.
You are the blanket fort hideout that no one
has figured out how to make . . . yet.

You are paper-mache beasts in a parade
with friends on a spring day.

You are not invisible.
You are not silent.
You are hand-painted signs,
    people marching together in the street
    for a more just world.

You are a portrait of farting cats, the paint still wet,
the favorite art of your ông nội and bà nội.
You are a story, shaped like a spinning globe.

You are condensed water floating as a cloud.
You are smoke from the incense
lit to honor our ancestors.

You are so colorful that no crayon box could hold you.
You are books spilling from a shelf overflowing,
the tales passed on and on.

You are skateboard, balance bike, kung fu *hi-yah!*,
   round ball through the hoop, rock climber,
   racket swinger, break-dancer.
You can do anything.

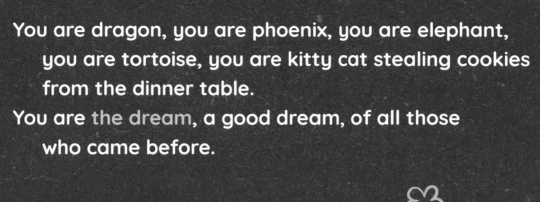

You are dragon, you are phoenix, you are elephant,
you are tortoise, you are kitty cat stealing cookies
from the dinner table.
You are the dream, a good dream, of all those
who came before.

You are a song whose melody has no border.
You are a song that needs no translation.
You are a song we can never stop singing
     against the silence.
You are a song that sings us, and we sing you.

AUTHOR'S NOTE

Unfortunately, anti-Asian violence is nothing new. It is a part of history, usually invisible. But during the COVID-19 pandemic, the sudden attention given to anti-Asian hate crimes allowed a window into that hurt, that struggle that Asian Americans are all too familiar with. Unfortunately, many Americans, of many different races, did not understand that racism against Asians is something that exists, so there was an erasure of our experience to go along with the violence. During that time, as a father to an Asian American child, there were so many emotions surging through me: anger, sadness, fear, resentment, exhaustion. But also, a glimmer of wanting to offer something hopeful, something that said, *yes, this happened to us, we must mark this history. At the same time, we must celebrate our lives* . . . life in the multitudes of how we exist, outside the boxes that we are all squeezed into. And so, this poem to young children came into being. To those who are not Asian American: thank you for taking the time and effort to read and learn about an experience outside of your own. To Asian Americans: you are not alone, and you are loved.

Thank you to the many Asian American friends who lived through this experience together, and who checked in with one another during these difficult times. Thank you to the kidlit community and everyone at Capstone, especially Dr. Sarah Park Dahlen and Krissy Mohn. And of course, thank you to Hannah Li, for the beautiful illustrations.

ABOUT THE AUTHOR

Bao Phi is an award-winning poet and children's book author. His stunning debut picture book with illustrator Thi Bui, *A Different Pond*, won a Caldecott Honor, a Charlotte Zolotow Award, an Asian/Pacific American Award for Literature, an Ezra Jack Keats Honor, a Boston Globe-Horn Book Honor, and numerous other awards and accolades. *You Are Life* is his fourth picture book. Bao is a single co-parent father, an arts administrator, and a book nerd.

ABOUT THE ILLUSTRATOR

Hannah Li is a New York-based illustrator from China. She graduated from Savannah College of Art and Design and creates illustrations for publishers, newspapers, and magazines such as the *The New York Times*, *The Washington Post,* and *Harper's Bazaar*. Hannah's work has been recognized by the Red Dot Award, *Communication Arts*, American Illustration, Society of Illustrators, *3x3*, and many more.

Printed and bound in the China. 4848